Big thanks to my family and friends for all of their support, input and encouragement. Special buzz to James, Charlie, Ailsa, Brian, Claire, Dave and Alison.

Published and Manufactured by
Softwood Books

**EU Responsible person: Maddy Glenn**
Office 2, Wharfside House, Prentice Road, Stowmarket, Suffolk, IP14 1RD
www.softwoodbooks.com, hello@softwoodbooks.com

**EU Rep:**
Authorised Rep Compliance Ltd., Ground Floor, 71 Lower Baggot Street, Dublin, D02 P593, Ireland
www.arccompliance.com, info@arccompliance.com

A CIP catalogue record for this book is available from the British Library

Text and Illustration Copyright © Nan Eshelby 2022
All rights reserved.

Without limiting the rights under copyright reserved above, no part of this publication may be reproduced, stored, or introduced into a retrieval system, or transmitted, in any form or by any means (electronic, mechanical, photocopying, recording or otherwise) without the prior written permission of both the copyright owners and the publisher of this book. This book was created without the use of artificial intelligence tools. The author does not grant permission for this manuscript to be used for training AI models or other machine learning purposes. The story, all names, characters, and incidents portrayed in this production are fictitious. No identification with actual persons (living or deceased), places, buildings, and products is intended or should be inferred.

ISBN 978-1-9168821-2-6

Maisie, Daisy and Mo met at school all together.

They knew right away they'd be firm friends forever.

A fabulous three, who make a great team,

They agree they love nature and to help is their dream.

Maisie, Daisy and Mo played hide and seek in the park. They discovered an oak tree with thick, lumpy bark.

They stood underneath, looking up to the sky, When suddenly they jumped hearing noises nearby.

A buzz it came down from a branch way up high.
Maisie whispered to them, "Let's investigate why".
The buzzing grew louder as the children went near.
A bee said, "I'm Bombus, there's nothing to fear".

Daisy whispered to Bombus, "Are you quite well?"
Bombus said feebly, "No, I've a sad tale to tell.
A shortage of flowers is making bees weak,
And if no one will help, the future is bleak".

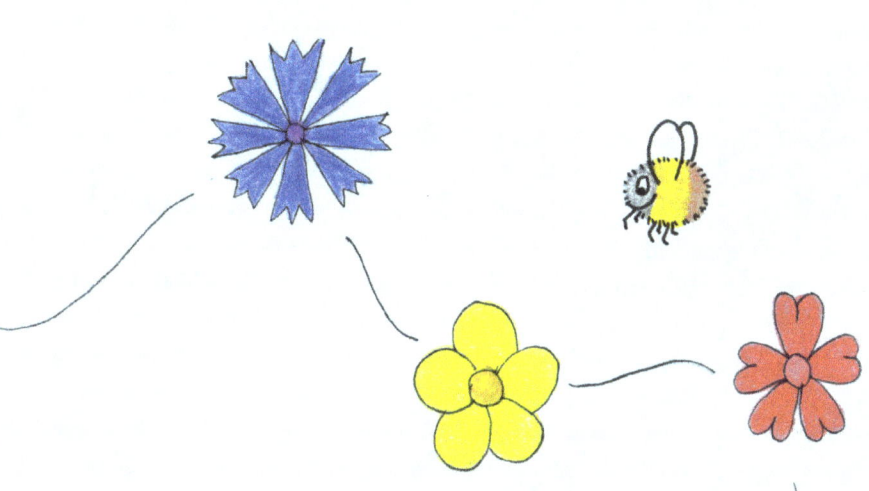

"Bees all need flowers for nectar and pollen:
These provide strength, but the numbers have fallen.
The path the bees fly from each flower head,
Is called a beeline and keeps the bees fed".

Bombus explained that although good for a ball,
An over trimmed lawn doesn't help bees at all.

So please ask your parents to let a section grow high,
And plant wildflowers to feed bees as they fly.

Maisie, Daisy and Mo cried out to each other,
"Let's all get to work and grow some wildflowers.
Each area we convert is like a small café.
Let's all act like chefs, keeping all the bees happy".

Maisie told Bombus they'd be ready with speed.
Mo asked their teacher where they could plant seed.
Daisy worked hard, finding lots of good flowers.
The team worked together, using all of their powers.

Campion, Cornflower, Catmint and Clover,
Buttercup, Bluebell, Rattle moreover,
Forget-me-not, Comfrey and Dead Nettle too,
So many to choose from, no problem for you.

Maisie, Daisy and Mo were ready to start:
Instructions, a spade, seed packet and heart.
Their teacher showed them a spare piece of ground.
Working hard with the spade, they dug up all round.

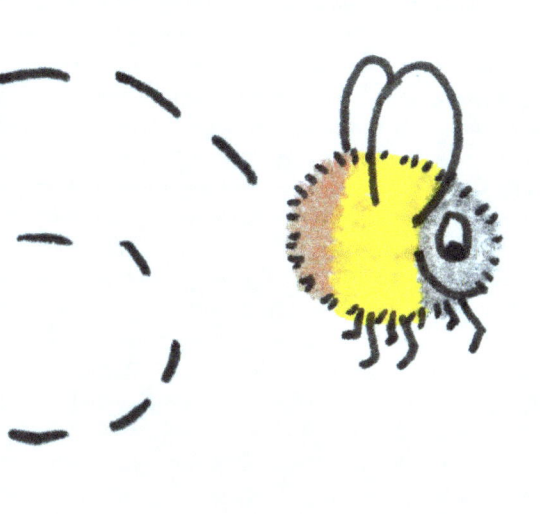

Mo took great care when sharing out seeds.

They knew they'd grow well, now there were no weeds.

A sprinkling of water was all to remain,

And home they all walked with a great sense of gain.

Each week they returned and checked out the ground. 
By week number three, green shoots they all found.
The arrival of spring filled them all with great glee.
Lots of bright flowers and healthy buzzing bees.

Flowers of pink, white, yellow and blue,
Short, tall and curly and shades of green too.
Bees of all sizes with fur and some stripes,
Were looking so healthy and full of new life.

Mo asked, "How do bees find new flowers to share?"

Bombus buzzed, "Bees can be different, but all do it with flare.

I can see patterns of scent on the flowers,

I think it's great and just one of my powers".

But honeybees are different and do a little dance
To help find new flowers, leaving nothing to chance.
With a wiggle and a waggle, the honeybees speak,
Giving directions to the flowers they seek.

"But that is not all!" Bombus said with great pride.
"There's other bee magic that I just can't hide".
He asked if they'd ever grown veggies or fruit,
And wondered how flowers can turn into food.

Bombus buzzed, "When a bee lands on a flower head,
They pick up some pollen on their hair as they tread.
Pollen falls off on the next flower they find.
It's called pollination and helps plants of all kinds".

Bombus and the team ask you to be kind,
Plant some wildflowers and make a beeline.
A window box, plant pot and hanging basket too,
All will work well, and bees will love you.

Growing a beeline would be grand, we agree.

We could celebrate together and bees buzz with great glee.

Bombus asks you to answer the call.

And now he is finished and says, "Thank you to all".

Why don't you draw your ideal flower garden, flowerpot, flower basket or window box here and don't forget to send in your coloured drawings and I will try to put them on the website

www.bombusthebee.com

Look out for Book 2, "Puddock's Pond".

Bombus has asked some of his Bombus friends to appear on the next two pages. Why don't you see if you can find any of these, or others, in your garden or local area? Bees can be a whole range of sizes; these pictures are not to scale but to give you an idea of what the bees look like. There are queen, worker and male bees and they may look slightly different. Try drawing your own.

**Tree Bumble Bee**
Bombus hypnorum

**Buff Tailed Bumble Bee**
Bombus terrestris
This picture shows a workerbee - only the Queen has a buff tail

**Common Carder Bee**
Bombus pascuorum

2mm

Smallest bee in the world is only 2mm long - the stingless bee

The size of the smallest and
largest bee is also shown,
but they are not found in the UK.

**Garden Bumble Bee**
Bombus hortorum
(can you tell the difference between
this bee and the Buff-tailed bee?))

**Red Tailed Bumble Bee**
Bombus lapidarius

**Early Bumble Bee**
Bombus pratorum

38mm

Largest bee is 38mm long - the Magachile Pluto

Maisie, Daisy and Mo have chosen some of their favourite bee facts for you here, but if you want to learn more there are loads of fabulous sources on the web.

"Bombus" is the family name (genus) of over 250 species of bumble bee.

In the UK there are around 270 species of bee of which there are at least 24 different species of bumblebee. World-wide there are over 25,000 recorded species of bee.

Some bees, like bumble bees and honeybees, are social bees that live in groups, but most bees (more than 90%) are solitary bees which means they live alone. Examples of some of the solitary bees you may see in your garden are the red mason bee and the Willughby's leaf cutter bee – have a look on the web and see what others you can find.

Some bees including bumble bees can give an extra big shake when on a flower, which releases extra pollen for the bees, and this is called Buzz Pollination.

Bees have Five Eyes. Two large eyes on the side of the head and three small simple eyes arranged in a triangle on the top of their heads. It is believed these three eyes help the bees use the sun to find their way to flowers and return home (navigate).

Many bumble bees that you will see are female worker bees and they collect the pollen and nectar from flowers and do most of the work in the nest. The male bees are called drones, they are generally there to find a queen bee. The queen bee's job is to lay the eggs, with a typical bumble bee colony being around 200 bees all originating from the one queen.

Some bees collect pollen from their hairy bodies and pack it onto their legs. If you look carefully, you can often see some bees with a big bundle of yellow pollen on each back leg that makes them look like they are wearing 'Pollen Pants'. Some solitary bees collect pollen on their stomachs.

## Bumble bee Life Cycle

The queen hibernates underground during the winter, emerging in spring to find a nest site. She then lays eggs that become worker bees and the nest begins.

The egg is laid and turns into a ...

Larva (grub) that eats a LOT of pollen and nectar provided by female bees. The grub quickly grows and at the right time it spins a cocoon and turns into a ...

Pupa where the BIG change (metamorphosis) to a bee happens. The young bee breaks out the cocoon and becomes an adult bee.

## How Bombus sees Flowers

Flowers have lots of different patterns on their surfaces that help to guide bees and other pollinators towards the flower's nectar, speeding up pollination.

These patterns include visual signals like lines pointing to the centre of the flower, or colour differences and even heat patterns – search for this title, 'Bees use invisible heat patterns to choose flowers'.

Flowers are thought to have different patterns of scent across their surface, and so a visiting bee might find that the centre of the flower smells differently to the edge of the petals. There is lots of good information on the web and here is an article – search for this title, 'Bumblebees distinguish floral scent patterns and can transfer these to corresponding visual patterns.'

Bees and other insects see in the ultraviolet spectrum of light, meaning they see in blues, greens and violet shades, and they cannot see red at all - to them it appears black. The flowers on page 17 show a representation of flowers as humans would see them and an illustration of what the bee might see.

## Some Information about Honeybees

Honeybees produce the honey that you see in the shops and honey can last a LONG time, even centuries if sealed! Some honey was found in Egyptian tombs which was 3000 years old and was still good to eat. The biggest reason is that the sugary honey is hygroscopic (contains almost no water), and bacteria and microorganisms do not like this and therefore don't grow. Keep your honey sealed and avoid moisture getting in and it should last you a long time. If your honey goes hard (crystallises) it is still fine to eat – and you can make it liquid again if you warm it gently.

Most honeybees live in hives and are cared for by humans.

Page 18 within this book that talks about the waggle dance that honeybees do. This dance tells the watching bees, about flowers, and the distance and direction the flowers are away from the hive. There is lots of good information on the web and here is an article, - search for this title, 'The flight paths of honeybees recruited by the waggle dance'.

www.ingramcontent.com/pod-product-compliance
Lightning Source LLC
LaVergne TN
LVHW081450070426
835510LV00015B/1862